SHORT TALES
Fairy Tales

Aladdin
and the
Lamp

Adapted by Shannon Eric Denton
Illustrated by Mike Dubisch

WAYLAND

WAYLAND

First published in 2013 by Wayland

Copyright © 2013 Wayland

Wayland
338 Euston Road
London NW1 3BH

Wayland Australia
Level 17/207 Kent Street
Sydney, NSW 2000

Adapted Text by Shannon Eric Denton
Illustrations by Mike Dubisch
Colours by Wes Hartman
Edited by Stephanie Hedlund
Interior Layout by Kristen Fitzner Denton and Alyssa Peacock
Book Design and Packaging by Shannon Eric Denton
Cover Design by Alyssa Peacock

Copyright © 2008 by Abdo Consulting Group

A cataloguing record for this title is available at the British Library.
Dewey number: 813.6

Printed in China

ISBN: 978 0 7502 7750 1

Wayland is a division of Hachette Children's Books, an Hachette UK company.
www.hachette.co.uk

In China, a young man named Aladdin played outside.

One day, a magician came to him.

The magician and Aladdin had a fun day in the city.

Then, the magician took Aladdin to see some beautiful gardens.

They walked until they had almost reached
the mountains.

Then the magician said some magic words.

The earth shook in front of them.

Soon, a stone with a brass
ring appeared.

The magician told Aladdin to go down the stairs, into a cave and get a lamp.

He gave Aladdin a ring and wished him luck.

Inside the cave, Aladdin saw beautiful trees.

He picked some of their fruit.

Then Aladdin found the lamp and returned to the entrance.

Aladdin decided he wouldn't give the magician the lamp until he was out of the cave.

This made the magician very angry.

He shouted some magic words and the cave door sealed.

Aladdin was locked inside.

He realized he had been tricked.

He wiped his hand and accidentally rubbed the ring.

When Aladdin rubbed the ring, a genie appeared!

The genie told Aladdin he would make his wishes come true.

Aladdin asked the genie to set him free and the genie did.

Aladdin ran home and told his mother everything.

When he showed her the fruit, he found they were jewels.

Aladdin's mother rubbed the lamp to clean it.

When she did, another genie appeared.

Aladdin asked the genie to get them something to eat.

Poof! Delicious food appeared on silver dishes.

Aladdin's mother enjoyed the meal.

But she wasn't happy about having a genie in the house.

She asked Aladdin to sell the lamp.

Instead, Aladdin sold the silver so they would have money.

There was more silver with every meal the genie brought them.

Aladdin and his mother did not have to worry about money again.

One day, Aladdin saw a beautiful princess.

He fell in love with her.

He decided he would marry her.

Aladdin needed permission from the Sultan to marry the princess.

Aladdin's mother agreed to help him.

She travelled to the Sultan's palace.

Aladdin's mother gave the jewels from the cave to the Sultan.

The Sultan was very pleased.

But the Sultan's assistant wanted his son to marry the princess.

The Sultan said, 'In three months I will decide who will marry my daughter.'

During the second month, Aladdin's mother heard news at the market.

The princess was marrying the assistant's son!

She rushed home and told Aladdin.

Aladdin ran to his magic lamp.

Aladdin asked the genie to make the assistant's son sleep outside in the freezing cold.

The genie made it so.

This went on for many nights.

Finally, the assistant's son ran away.

Aladdin's mother returned to the palace.

The Sultan decided to give Aladdin one more test.

The Sultan said, 'Your son must send me forty baskets full of jewels. They must be carried by eighty attendants. Then he may marry my daughter.'

Aladdin again used his magic lamp.

The Sultan was surprised.

He said that Aladdin could marry the princess.

Upon hearing the good news, Aladdin asked the genie for a horse and servants.

Aladdin rode towards the palace.

Along the way, his attendants gave out gold.

When the Sultan saw him, he said Aladdin would marry the princess that very day.

Aladdin told the Sultan he wanted to build the princess a palace first.

The Sultan was very happy.

At home Aladdin said to the genie, 'Build me a palace of the finest marble.'

The genie immediately began his work.

The palace was finished the next day.

The princess set out for Aladdin's palace.

She was very happy when she saw Aladdin.

The two were married that night.

It was the most beautiful wedding the kingdom had ever seen.

Aladdin and the princess lived happily for many years.

One day, the magician heard word of this happy kingdom.

He was angry that Aladdin had the magic lamp.

The magician hurried to the kingdom.

He wanted to steal the lamp.

The magician bought a dozen new lamps.

He tricked the princess into trading the magic lamp.

The magician then used the genie to steal the princess and the palace!

Aladdin promised to save the princess.

He rubbed the magician's magic ring.

The genie took Aladdin to the palace.

Aladdin quickly found the princess and the magician.

He bravely beat the magician with quick thinking.

Aladdin took back his lamp.

Aladdin asked the genie to carry him, the princess and the palace back to China.

Soon, the princess and Aladdin were home again!

They lived the rest of their lives in peace.

SHORT TALES
Fables

Titles in the Short Tales Fables series:

The Ants and the Grasshopper

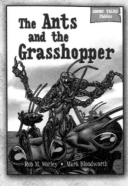

978 0 7502 7756 3

The Boy Who Cried Wolf

978 0 7502 7757 0

The Fox and the Grapes

978 0 7502 7758 7

The Lion and the Mouse

978 0 7502 7783 9

The Tortoise and the Hare

978 0 7502 7784 6

The Town Mouse and the Country Mouse

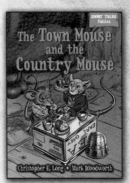

978 0 7502 7785 3

WAYLAND
www.waylandbooks.co.uk

Follow us on Twitter @waylandbooks | Find us on Facebook Wayland Books

SHORT TALES
Fairy Tales

Titles in the Short Tales Fairy Tales series:

Aladdin and the Lamp

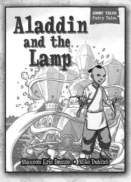

978 0 7502 7750 1

Beauty and the Beast

978 0 7502 7752 5

Jack and the Beanstalk

978 0 7502 7751 8

Puss in Boots

978 0 7502 7754 9

Sleeping Beauty

978 0 7502 7755 6

The Little Mermaid

978 0 7502 7753 2

WAYLAND

www.waylandbooks.co.uk

Follow us on Twitter @waylandbooks | Find us on Facebook Wayland Books